Water Tales

ALICE HOFFMAN

Two Novels

Aquamarine & Indigo

EGMONT

Aquarmarine
To Carol and Allison DeKnight
and to Jo Ann who believed in mermaids

Indigo
To those born under the signs of water,
especially to Wolfe Martin

EGMONT

We bring stories to life

Aquamarine first published in Great Britain 2003 by Egmont Books Limited
First published in the USA 2001 by Scholastic Inc.
Indigo first published in Great Britain 2004 by Egmont Books Limited
First published in the USA 2002 by Scholastic Inc.
All rights reserved.
Published by arrangment with Scholastic Inc.
557 Broadway, New York, NY 10012, USA

This omnibus edition published 2005
by Egmont Books Limited
239 Kensington High Street
London W8 6SA

Text copyright © 2001, 2002 Alice Hoffman
Illustration copyright © 2003, 2004 Lee Gibbons

The moral rights of the author and illustrator have been asserted

ISBN 1 4052 1831 2

1 3 5 7 9 10 8 6 4 2

A CIP catalogue record for this title is available from the British Library

Printed and bound in Great Britain by the CPI Group

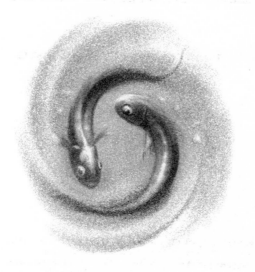

Aquamarine

CHAPTER ONE

At the Capri Beach Club, every day was hotter and hotter until the asphalt in the parking lot began to bubble. Snow cones and ice-cream sandwiches melted as soon as they were removed from the snack shop's freezers, and the sand burned the feet of anyone who dared to walk along the beach at noon. The heat popped and crackled and wouldn't let up. It didn't matter if there was an evening storm with high winds and buckets of pouring rain; by morning the sky was once again blue and clear. People began to sit in the shade, and after a while most of them stayed home in their cool, air-conditioned rooms. Even those families who had been coming to the beach club for years gave up their memberships and found other ways to while away the scorching days of August.

The Capri had been more run-down every season, but this year was clearly the worst. No wonder the owner was closing the club at the end of the month. Weeds were sprouting in the tennis courts, beach umbrellas were filled with holes, seagulls had taken over the pool area, nesting on chaise lounges and sipping chlorinated water. The lifeguards had gone out on strike in July, and had never returned. Even the cafeteria had closed down – the windows were boarded over, the door nailed shut – leaving only the snack shop, run by Raymond, who would soon be going off to college in Miami and was far too busy reading to fix a sandwich or fetch a glass of lemonade.

The only people who still came to the Capri every day were two twelve-year-old girls and they didn't mind the heat one bit. Hailey and Claire had lived next door to

each other and been best friends all their lives. Unlike most people in town, they wanted this summer to go on forever, no matter how humid or hot. They both hoped that August would continue beyond the confines of its thirty-one days, in a blaze of sunshine and heat. These girls had stopped looking at calendars. They didn't wear watches. They shut their eyes when the first star appeared in the sky. The reason they wished every day to be the same was that at the end of the month, Claire would be moving to Florida with her grandparents and Hailey would be left behind.

'Don't talk about it,' Hailey said

whenever Claire brought up the subject. 'Don't even think about it.'

For although Hailey thought nothing of leaping from the highest diving platform or swimming so far out to sea that she disappeared from sight, she was easily frightened by other things – a future she couldn't control, for instance, or the notion that a lifelong friendship might be lost at the end of the week when the Capri closed down for good and Claire moved away.

As for Claire, she was quiet and shy and as afraid of water as Hailey was drawn to it. She had lost both her parents in an accident on the expressway, and ever since, her vision of the world had darkened. She'd become

skittish, forsaking those things which brought other girls joy. Swimming, for instance, made her so nervous she refused to dip her toes into shallow water, not even on a burning hot day.

Between the two friends, Claire had always been the problem solver. She was the sort of girl who could take an old dress, stitch a hem, add a sash, and wind up with an outfit that made it seem as though she'd just walked out of the finest store. Given a patch of bare ground and some flower seeds, she would soon have the prettiest garden on the block. But now Claire was faced with a problem she couldn't solve.

She had begged and she'd pleaded,

Aquamarine

promising to never again ask for another favour if only they could stay, but her grandparents had already sold their house and rented an apartment in Florida, right on the beach. As if an oceanfront view mattered to Claire. As if she ever wanted to go to any beach but the one at the Capri where she and Hailey had spent every summer of their lives.

Both girls knew that things changed, sometimes for the worse. Claire had lost her parents and Hailey's mother and father had been divorced, and now her mother worked long hours and hadn't any time to have fun. But the Capri had always stayed the same, a place to hold on to even in the darkest

days of winter when snow piled up by their back doors.

All summer long, the girls had been dropped off at the Capri by Hailey's mum on her way to work, and picked up at six o'clock sharp by Claire's grandfather, Maury. Maury was so happy to be moving to Florida that all the neighbours agreed he now looked at least ten years younger, much better than he had last winter when he'd broken his leg after slipping on a patch of slick ice. He'd needed to use a wheelchair until the following spring, and it was this accident which had convinced Claire's grandmother it was time to relocate to a place where winter was no longer a concern for what she called rickety old bones.

'What's new, Susie Q's?' Maury would always say when the two friends traipsed through the heat waves that rose up in the parking lot at the end of the day. Time was speeding forward regardless of their wishes. No matter how slowly they dragged their feet, every day was still twenty-four hours closer to moving day.

Whenever they left the Capri, they'd see Raymond's motorbike parked in the shadows of the breezeway. But there wasn't another vehicle in sight. Who would want to spend their precious summer days at a beach club that had become a disaster area? Beyond a wire fence, several bulldozers were

9

already at work tearing down the playground where the swings had long ago rusted into place. Still, it hadn't been that many summers since Hailey and Claire had ridden those swings into the sky, up through the heat waves and the white clouds, convinced they had all the time in the world.

Now, in the last days of the Capri, time seemed to be their enemy. Sometimes, when they looked into the mirror in the changing room of the cabana, where bathing suits and towels were stored, they didn't even look like themselves anymore. Their legs were too long, their arms too rangy, their hair cut too short to be pulled into ponytails or braids.

Each day when Claire's grandfather

asked, 'What's new, Susie Q's?' the girls always responded, 'Nothing' in voices so glum, anyone would think they had no hope whatsoever for what the future might bring. By next summer, the Capri would be a bird sanctuary, and although the girls were happy for the birds, they didn't understand why this one piece of their lives couldn't go on as before.

Once the bulldozers started in on the wooden cabanas, once they destroyed the pool and the patio and the snack bar, wasn't it possible that Claire would no longer remember summers spent at the Capri with her parents? Would Hailey still recall how her father took her swimming in the farthest

waves when her mum and dad were still married? When the Capri was gone, maybe they would forget each other as well. They'd grow up and be just like all those other people who didn't know what it meant to have your best friend living right next door, grown-ups who had no idea of what it was like to have someone understand you so well they could tell what you were thinking even before you spoke aloud.

The last days of August were identical, blistering mornings fading into white-hot afternoons. At the start of the day, the girls sat by the pool, trailing their fingers in the water and shooing the seagulls away. At lunch time, they bothered Raymond, who seemed much too handsome to be as nice as he was. He never minded when Hailey and Claire sat at the counter for hours, drinking lemonade and watching him read. In past summers, there had been flocks of teenaged girls hanging around Raymond, but all those girls' families had joined town pools or rented summer houses, and only Hailey and Claire remained to admire him. Late in the afternoon, when it was almost time to go, the girls walked along the beach. Sometimes Hailey went in for a swim to cool off, but Claire stayed on the shore, adding to her collection of stones and shells.

And so every day blended into the next,

13

until one morning there was a storm with gusts of sixty miles an hour and extraordinarily high tides. The girls had to stay home that day, and they shivered at the nearness of September. They barely said a word all afternoon. That night, in houses right next door to each other, neither one could sleep. The wind was so strong, it knocked on the rooftops and rattled the stars up above. Both Hailey and Claire had the feeling that something was about to happen, in spite of how much they wanted their lives to remain the same.

When they arrived at the beach club the next morning, they found that the storm had left its mark. The wooden paths were littered with purple snails. Starfish and scallops were trapped in the fountain at the centre of the patio and the snack bar was missing its roof. The pool had been roped off and a NO SWIMMING sign had been hastily installed by the owner, who hardly even bothered to visit the club anymore.

The water in the pool was as thick as soup. Seaweed clogged up the filter. Barnacles clung to the blue and white tiles and luminous moon jellyfish slowly drifted by. Hailey, who had learned how to swim in this very pool when she was only a toddler, was outraged at what a mess it had become.

'What difference does it make?' Claire

15

said. 'After next Saturday, they'll drain the pool and bulldoze it, too.'

Even though she had never dared swim in the pool, there were tears in Claire's eyes as she gazed into the murky waters. For the first time in a long while, she had no idea of what to do next. Maybe that was why Hailey ducked under the ropes to take a closer look.

Hailey had always been fearless and a little too curious for her own good, but she'd always had Claire there behind her, urging her on, concocting their plans. She stuck her toes in the water and wondered what would become of her once she was all by herself. A nobody, a nothing, with no one to talk to and no one to call in the middle of the night

16

when she heard her mother crying, or when a stray dog knocked over a garbage can. Hailey stood at the very edge of the pool. Before Claire could tell her it wasn't a good idea, before she lost all of her courage, she dove in.

Hailey was such a good diver, there wasn't a sound when she entered the water, just a series of ripples circling out from the centre of the pool. Claire quickly clambered over the ropes and ran to the spot where Hailey had last been standing, making certain to hold on to the railing so she wouldn't fall in herself. Claire had spent her whole life worrying that her friend would do something foolish and jump in

17

head first where she didn't belong, and now Hailey had done exactly that.

The strange, cloudy water made Claire more nervous about the pool than she usually was. She had never even learned the Dead Man's Float, which, when you really thought about it, wasn't the most comforting name. You never could tell what might happen in the water. You'd have to have faith in yourself to dive in, and that was something Claire didn't possess.

Sixty seconds later, Hailey came bursting back through the surface, sputtering and shaking with cold. She dragged herself up the rungs of the ladder, too chilled and breathless to speak. In the deep end of the pool, the moon jellyfish rode the current through strands of brown seaweed.

Best friends don't need to be told when something extraordinary has happened, and this was the case with Hailey and Claire. One look, and Claire knew that her friend's swim had been anything but ordinary.

'What did you see?' Claire asked. 'What's down there?'

Hailey didn't say, *You'll never believe me*, which is what she would have told anyone else. She knew Claire would believe her, no matter what, so she whispered the name of what she'd seen in the deep end of the pool where everything was hazy and dim. Claire held even more tightly to the railing, lest she

19

fall in and be faced with the creature Hailey had seen, because she absolutely, positively, without a doubt, believed.

On this day when Claire's grandfather asked, 'What's new Susie Q's?' the girls stared at each other, eyes shining. 'Nothing,' they said together, the way best friends often do. Of course, what they really meant was that they weren't quite sure. What they meant was that for the first time in a very long while, they couldn't wait for morning to come.

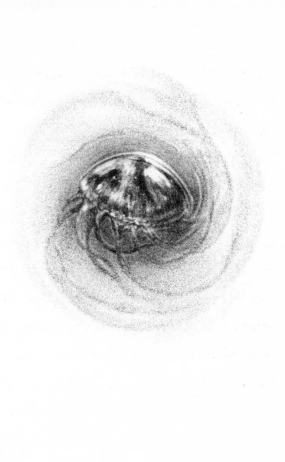

CHAPTER TWO

The next day, as soon as they got out of
Hailey's mother's car in the parking lot,
Hailey was the one who took charge. After
all, she'd been the one to see the mermaid
at the bottom of the pool, huddled in a
murky corner, her long hair streaming.
Claire wouldn't have ventured into the

water for any reason, not even to see such a wondrous being.

As they went through the entranceway to the Capri, Hailey handed her friend a jar she'd stored in her backpack. Claire held the jar up to the light and tried her best to figure out what the slippery-looking things were inside.

'Herring,' Hailey told her when Claire couldn't venture a guess. 'It's a kind of marinated fish. I found it in the back of the pantry. Mermaids must get hungry. All we need to do is hide behind the diving board, and when she comes to the surface to eat, we can study her.'

'Good plan,' Claire said. At any other

24

time, Claire would have been the one to come up with the plans, but lately she'd been up half the night, thinking about how her sweaters and boots would be pointless in Florida, and how the leaves wouldn't change in the fall, and how it would be summer all year long.

Hailey, herself, was somewhat surprised to find that she'd actually been the one with the ideas. 'You really think it's a good plan?' she asked uncertainly.

'Excellent,' Claire said, although she, too, was surprised at how quickly everything was changing already, even though it was still the same.

* * *

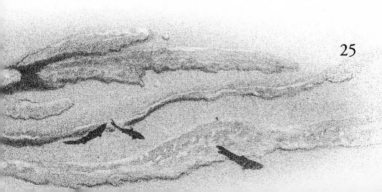

After they'd sprinkled the herring in the pool, the girls waited behind the diving board. Jellyfish floated on the surface of the water, and a few bubbles arose up from the deep, but there was no sign of the mermaid. Hours passed and the girls didn't move. Time was so slow, and the air was so hot, they almost fell asleep.

When they didn't show up at the snack bar for lunch, Raymond came looking for them.

'What happened to my only customers?' he asked. 'I was worried. I thought the seagulls had carried you away.'

Raymond sat on the edge of a lounge chair and gazed into the pool. He was so

handsome that for a few minutes the girls forgot there was a mermaid nearby.

'What a disaster,' Raymond said, looking around the beach club. 'I should have taken a different job this summer, but I guess I got used to this place.' When he'd first come to the Capri, he'd been the assistant to the assistant cook at the snack bar, and at lunch time they'd all had to work like crazy just to fill the orders of hamburgers and sandwiches and fries. There were crowds of people and the air smelled like coconut-scented sunscreen. Not a single one of the chaise lounges would have been empty on a beautiful day such as this. But that was all in the past.

27

'I don't want it to end,' Raymond admitted.

'We know,' the girls said at the very same time. 'Neither do we.'

'Don't forget to come by and have a lemonade. My treat,' Raymond said as he started back to the snack bar. 'After all, there are only a few days left to the summer.'

Hailey had always noticed that Raymond often read two books at a time, and Claire had always noticed that he was so kindhearted, he fed day-old bread to the seagulls that followed him as though he were their favourite person on earth. Now they both could tell he was almost as sad as they were about the Capri closing.

Aquamarine

The girls had been watching Raymond so intently, it was a while before they realised that a mermaid had surfaced at the shallow end of the pool. Her hair was pale and silvery and her nails were a shimmering blue. Between each finger there was a thin webbing, of the sort you might find on a newborn seal or a duck.

'What are you two staring at?' the mermaid said, when she turned and saw the girls gaping.

Her voice was as cool and fresh as bubbles rising from the ocean. She was as beautiful as a pearl, with a faint turquoise tinge to her skin and eyes so blue they were the exact same colour as the deepest sea. But her watery beauty didn't mean the mermaid knew her manners.

'Stop looking at me,' she demanded, as she splashed at the girls. 'Go away!'

The mermaid's name was Aquamarine and she was much ruder than most creatures you might find at sea. At sixteen, she was the youngest of seven sisters, and had always been spoiled. She'd been indulged and cared for and allowed to act up in ways no self-respecting mermaid ever would.

Her disagreeable temperament certainly hadn't improved after spending two nights in the pool, tossed there like a stone or a sea urchin at the height of the terrible storm.

Aquamarine

Chlorine had seeped into her sensitive skin and silver scales dropped from her long, graceful tail. She hadn't eaten anything more than a mouthful of that horrible herring the girls had strewn into the pool.

'You heard me,' Aquamarine said to Hailey and Claire, who were mesmerised by her gleaming tail and by the way the mermaid could dive so quickly, she disappeared in a luminous flash. When she surfaced through the seaweed she was not pleased to see they were still there. 'Scram,' she said. 'Stop bothering me.'

The mermaid glided into the deep end of the pool, the better to see Raymond at the snack bar. She had been watching him ever since she found herself stranded in the pool. His was the first human face she saw. She gazed at him with a bewildered expression, the sure sign of a mermaid in love.

'They're closing the Capri at the end of the week. The pool is going to be drained,' Hailey called to Aquamarine. 'You're going to have to go back to where you came from by Saturday.'

The mermaid started to pay attention. 'Where will the people go?'

'What people?' Hailey said. 'Everyone's already gone except for us.'

'Not exactly.' Claire nodded toward Raymond. 'Not everyone.'

Aquamarine

'He's going on Saturday, too,' Hailey said. 'He's leaving for college.'

As soon as Aquamarine heard this, she began to cry blue, freshwater tears. No mermaid wants to fall in love with a human, but it was already too late for poor Aquamarine to be sensible. A sensible mermaid never would have wandered away from her sisters during a storm the way Aquamarine had.

As for Hailey and Claire, they couldn't know that a mermaid in love is far more irrational than a jellyfish and more stubborn than a barnacle. 'You'll just have to go back to the ocean,' they advised her.

'I'm not going anywhere.'

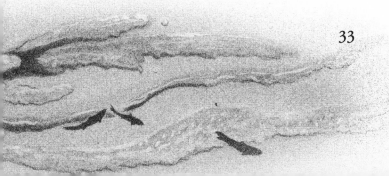

Aquamarine's pale complexion flushed blue as she pouted. 'I won't leave before I meet him.'

Up at the snack bar, Raymond was whistling a tune as he cleaned up the counter. Aquamarine tilted her head to listen, hearkening to what she clearly believed was the most beautiful melody anyone had ever been privileged to hear, either on land or at sea.

'Oh,' she sighed as she watched Raymond. Her elbows rested on the edge of the pool. Her sea-blue eyes were dreamy. 'If he only knew how I felt about him.'

'I really don't think he's your type,' Claire said as politely as she could.

Aquamarine

Aquamarine looked stricken. She had never been denied anything she wanted. 'Of course he is,' she said.

'Well, for one thing, he lives on land,' Hailey reminded the mermaid.

'You are both so mean,' Aquamarine cried. 'You're meaner than my sisters, and probably just as jealous.'

Since she'd been swept up by the storm and set down at the Capri, Aquamarine had felt a taste of freedom. More important than the terrible food and the chlorinated pool was the idea that she could do whatever she pleased. She tossed her head and fixed the girls with her sea-blue eyes. 'No one can tell me what to do any more. Not my sisters and certainly not you. Anyway, it's too late. I've already made up my mind. I'm staying right here for as long as I want to. And no one can tell me otherwise!'

At the end of the day, the girls ran to Claire's grandfather's car and when he said, 'What's new, Susie Q's?' they let out a gale of giggles, convinced that no one would believe that they'd stumbled upon a mermaid who refused to behave. When they got to Claire's grandparents' house, they raced past the half-packed boxes in the living room and looked through the crates of books in Claire's room, hoping to find a solution for Aquamarine's predicament. Although they discovered references to many unusual creatures of the deep, from dolphins that were said to rescue lost sailors to sea-serpents twice the size of a whale, they couldn't unearth a single bit of advice on what to do with a mermaid who'd fallen in love.

That night, the girls had dinner at Hailey's house. Through the kitchen window they could see the new people, the ones who'd bought Claire's grandparents' house. They were getting a final tour of the yard to ensure that once they moved in they would know how to best care for the garden. They'd be aware of which plants would bloom to be day lilies and which ones would forever remain weeds. A red-haired girl of twelve trailed after the new people. She looked uncertain and lonely and she stopped to smell the roses that Claire's grandmother had planted beside the back door.

'Maybe she'll be your new best friend,' Claire said.

'I'm never even going to talk to her,' Hailey assured Claire.

'Never?' Claire said hopefully.

'Not unless there's a fire and I have to shout for her to get out of the house.'

That night Claire was thinking about what might happen if there ever really was a fire; how Hailey would run over in her nightgown and pound her fists on the door to wake everyone and save them, and

38

how the red-haired girl would always be grateful, and how no one would even remember that Claire had ever lived in that same house. Claire was so wrapped up in trying to forecast the future, that she wasn't her usual problem-solving self. Frankly, she wasn't herself at all. She nearly jumped out of her chair when the phone rang. It was the friends' special signal: one ring, then hang up, then call right back again.

Claire went into the kitchen to answer the phone. She looked through the window and across the yard to where Hailey was, in her own kitchen. All night, Claire had been wondering who she would be without

Hailey to take up her plans and turn them into actions. In case of a fire, would Claire be courageous enough to knock on the door of a burning house?

Hailey waved across the yard. 'I found an encyclopedia of mythical creatures.' Hailey held a red book up to the window for Claire to see.

'She's not mythological,' Claire reminded her friend.

'Well, whatever she is, this book says that no mermaid can remain on land. The longest survival on record was one week in a circus and on the seventh day that mermaid dried up from head to tail. Nothing was left but a pile of green dust.'

Aquamarine

'What can we do?' Claire said. 'She won't listen to us.'

Unless Hailey was mistaken, Claire was actually asking for advice. Now that the responsibility rested with her, there was really no choice but for Hailey to come up with a plan, and that's exactly what she did.

'All we need to do is get her what she wants,' Hailey decided. 'Then she'll have to listen.'

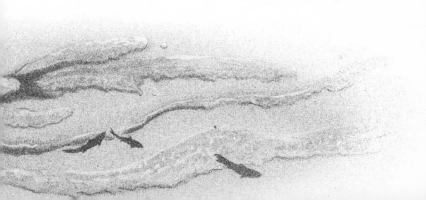

CHAPTER THREE

Raymond was packing his books when they found him. He had worked at the Capri for four summers, and although he still hadn't figured out how to cook a hamburger without burning the meat, he'd read one hundred and twenty-two books during his time at the beach. All the same, he wasn't sure he'd read quite enough to go to college. The future seemed like a cloud that day, the black, stormy kind it was impossible to see through, the sort that could make a person believe that blue skies would never again return.

But Raymond's worrying was interrupted when the girls ran to the snack counter to tell him they needed his help. They had a cousin visiting, they told him, from overseas, which wasn't so far from the truth. To make certain their cousin wouldn't be bored, the girls wanted Raymond to have dinner with her the following night.

'How can you have the same cousin?' Raymond was confused. 'I didn't even think you were related.'

46

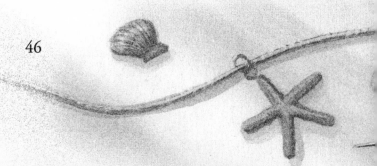

Aquamarine

'It's through marriage,' Hailey said because she'd heard other people use that excuse to explain complicated family relationships.

'And divorce,' Claire added, because she'd heard that as well.

'Anyway, she's a very distant cousin,' Hailey said. 'We just want her to have a good time while she's here. All you have to do is show up in the cafeteria at six o'clock tomorrow night.'

After Raymond had agreed to the dinner, Claire began to wonder how Hailey kept coming up with all these ideas, one after another, as if they just popped into her

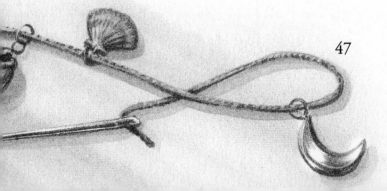

head. Now, for instance, Hailey raced to the pool, where she sat with her feet dangling in the shallow end. She took a can of tuna and an opener from her backpack, having remembered that the mermaid would be hungry.

'Good thinking,' Claire said to her friend.

Claire sat beside Hailey, but was careful not to hang her feet over the edge of the pool. She looked into the water, and gingerly dipped one toe in. It wasn't quite as cold as they'd thought it might be. Just to be safe, she held on to the concrete.

When they told Aquamarine of her date with Raymond, she let out a shriek of

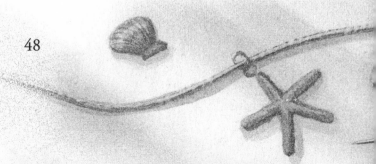

joy that chased the perching seagulls into the sky.

'You only have to promise one thing,' the girls reminded her. 'After tomorrow, you'll go.'

Aquamarine begged and cried until the pool was awash with blue tears which stained the moon jellyfish turquoise and indigo, but the girls would not change their minds.

'We're doing this for your own good,' they said. 'We want what's best for you.'

Without saltwater, they told her, Aquamarine's skin would soon dry up until her fresh face became grainy as sand, her beautiful pale hair would curl like seaweed,

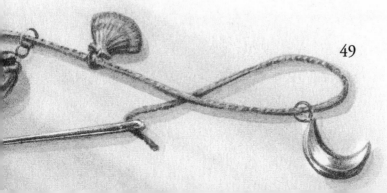

49

her tail would turn limp and dull. Already, her time away from the ocean had caused her to fade, so that when she blushed or was angry she turned silver rather than blue. The webbing between her fingers had fallen away, and her hands looked like those of any ordinary girl. Out in the waves, her six sisters were calling for her. They missed her and worried and at high tide they came dangerously close to shore in their search.

'All right,' Aquamarine said finally. 'I promise I'll go.'

Upon making this vow, the mermaid cried even harder.

'Cheer up,' Claire said. 'You'll always

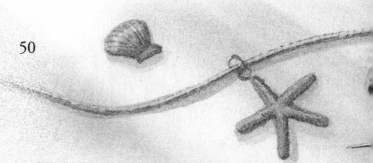

remember the night you had together.'

But now that Aquamarine was to get her heart's desire, she was nervous. 'What if he doesn't like me?' she wondered.

Although at first Aquamarine had been happy enough to be free of her sisters, the truth was she'd been coddled and protected for so long that she couldn't seem to figure anything out on her own. She had never even braided her long, silver hair, for there had always been her sisters' twelve hands to turn the strands into plaits.

'I look dreadful,' the mermaid said. Indeed, her hair was stringy and her fingertips were puckered and pale. 'I don't even have anything to wear.'

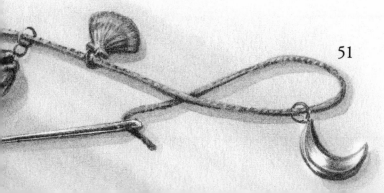

51

'Claire can solve that problem,' Hailey said.

'I can?' Claire really hadn't a clue as to what she could do to help out. How could she think straight? Her whole life was packed up and sitting in her grandparents' garage. When the moving van came to cart everything away, she wasn't sure she'd even know who she was anymore.

'I'll get one of my mother's dresses,' Hailey said, 'and you can make it beautiful, the way you always do.'

Although Claire was pleased by the compliment, she was thoughtful as well. 'One problem,' she whispered. 'What do we do about the tail?'

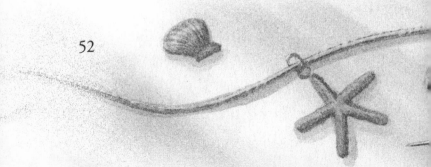

Aquamarine

'Oh, the tail.'

The girls studied Aquamarine solemnly, staring until she covered her face with her hands.

'I'm horrid,' the mermaid despaired. 'I'd be better off falling in love with a dolphin or a shark. It's no use. It's hopeless. I might as well stay in this pool until they drain it and take me away.'

At that, Aquamarine sunk to the depths of the murky water. All the girls could see of her were little bubbles rising and popping as they hit the air.

'She's probably right.' Claire crouched down to peer into the deep end. She splashed her hands in the cold salty water,

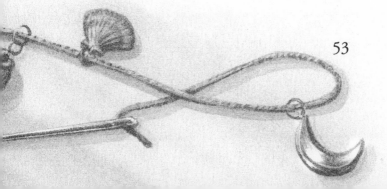

hoping to call Aquamarine to the surface, but there was no response. Not a flicker, not a fin, not a face. 'It *is* hopeless. How could we ever hide her tail?'

'I've got it!' Hailey said. She couldn't have been more pleased with herself, not even if she'd managed a perfect swan dive. 'We'll say she's had an accident. She can't walk, just like your grandfather last winter.'

That afternoon they ran to Claire's grandfather's car in the parking lot, threw themselves inside, and begged to borrow Maury's wheelchair before he could begin to get out the words *Susie Q's*.

'Please,' the girls cried. 'It's for a friend, and you don't need it any more.'

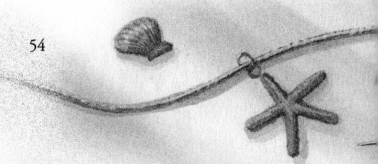

aquamarine

When they got home, Claire's grandfather unearthed the wheelchair from the bottom of a pile of odds and ends set out for the moving men. Hailey's mother found a blue dress at the back of her closet that she had worn to a dance years ago, before Hailey had even been born.

Later that night, after the grown-ups had gone to sleep, Claire went to her room and opened the last box she had packed. This was where she kept all the treasures of summers past. There were angel wings and creamy oyster shells, tiny starfish and pink rocks. She stitched every one on to the blue dress, so that the fabric shone in the moonlight, sighing as though it had just

been fished out of the sea. Claire had decided not to think about the fact that in twenty-four hours she would have to set off for Florida. She wasn't going to think about what it would be like when there was no one next door to make secret phone calls to late at night, and no one to wave at through the open kitchen windows.

'It's perfect,' Hailey declared over the phone when Claire held the dress up to the window for her to see. The blue fabric moved in the breeze. 'He'll fall in love with her the minute he sees her.'

Both girls were so sure of this they wouldn't have been the least surprised to discover that all night long Raymond

56

Aquamarine

dreamed of high tides and deep blue seas, and that at the bottom of the Capri's pool, where the moon jellyfish glittered like stars, Aquamarine braided her long, silvery hair and tried her best to ignore her sisters' song, which reached up from the ocean to call her home.

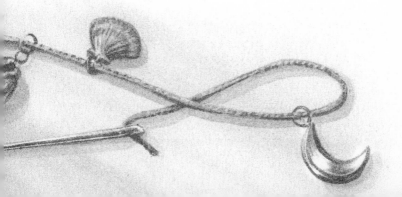

CHAPTER FOUR

They decided to tell Claire's grandfather. For one thing, he wasn't like most grown-ups – he actually listened to what they had to say – and for another, the girls needed to stay at the Capri until nine, in order to take Aquamarine home from her date with Raymond. After they had recounted the story of the mermaid in love, Maury didn't say a word. He didn't say he'd never heard such nonsense before. He didn't say, *Maloney baloney*, which he sometimes shouted out when he didn't believe some bit of news he heard on the radio. The way he listened made Claire realise how fortunate she was to have him as her grandfather. He even drove them to the beach that morning, telling Hailey's mum he wanted to chauffeur the girls as a way to say good-bye, since the next day was Saturday, their last day at the club. Although this excuse was true enough, the other reason he drove wasn't mentioned: the wheelchair fit neatly into the trunk of his car.

Aquamarine

'I know you won't believe this,' Maury said when they got to the beach, 'but you're not the only ones who've ever seen a mermaid. I've spotted several myself down in Florida, although I admit I've never gotten to know one personally. When you think about it, you are two lucky girls.'

Maury told them to have a good time and not to worry. He'd be waiting in the parking lot at nine and, like most people who've seen mermaids, even from a distance, he could be depended on not to tell.

Hailey and Claire borrowed a hammer they found in one of the abandoned cabanas to open the boarded-up cafeteria. Once inside, they swept the layer of sand from the floor and dusted the cobwebs off tables and chairs. After that was accomplished, they set out the dinner Hailey had thought to bring along, a carefully planned menu of tuna-fish sandwiches, seaweed salad, and sardines on toast. There was spring water for Raymond and a glass of saltwater, perfectly chilled for Aquamarine.

When they got to the pool, they saw that the water had turned so murky that the shallow end resembled a tidal pool. Purple snails climbed the metal rungs of the stairs and seagulls dived to scoop up the little silver fish that swam past the mosaic tiles. Aquamarine was waiting for them. She was even more faded than she'd been the day before, her tail withering to white, her complexion turning chalky, but when she saw the dress they held up, she turned blue with delight.

'Come and get me out,' the mermaid demanded, and then she thought better of what she had said. 'Please,' she amended. 'Help me.'

'How do we get her out?' Claire asked Hailey.

'We have to go into the pool and carry her,' Hailey said. 'There is no other way.'

Claire turned cold at the very thought. 'But I don't swim,' she reminded her friend.

'You don't have to,' Hailey assured

65

her. 'All you have to do is wade into the shallow end.'

And so they went into the pool slowly, and only as deep as their waists. But even in three feet of water, Claire was fearful, especially when the moon jellies floated near. Still, the girls managed to carry Aquamarine out, and they lifted her on to the wheelchair. After that, they helped her get dressed in one of the abandoned cabanas. When they cleaned off the mirror and Aquamarine finally saw her reflection, she made a sound that was somewhere between laughter and a wave breaking.

'Oh, thank you,' she said, completely

delighted. 'I look like a real girl.'

As they wheeled Aquamarine to the cafeteria, the sun began to set. Thankfully, the air was turning cooler – still being on land had begun to affect the mermaid. Out of saltwater, she was rapidly drying up. Claire had to collect the trail of scales that were shedding from her silvery tail.

'What if he doesn't like me?' Aquamarine worried. 'What if I'm all wrong?'

But she had nothing to worry about. Hailey and Claire knew that for certain because the moment Raymond saw her, he looked as though he were drowning.

'She's your cousin?' he said to the girls. 'I've never seen anyone like her before.'

'That's because she isn't like anyone else. She's special,' Hailey told Raymond. 'And she's had an accident, sort of, so don't ask her to dance.'

Hailey and Claire waited outside on the patio. They pulled up lounge chairs and listened to the murmur of voices and the beautiful sound of Aquamarine's watery laughter. Up in the summer sky, there were so many stars a person would never be able to count them all. Claire wondered if there would be the exact same stars in Florida, and if when she gazed out her window she'd still be looking at the same constellations that Hailey saw.

'That new girl with the red hair isn't so

horrible,' Claire said. 'Her name is Susanna. Susie Q. You get it?' The new people had come back again, and Claire had showed Susanna the room that would soon be hers. 'She's actually nice.'

'I don't care,' Hailey said. 'It doesn't really matter to me if she's nice or not. I'm never talking to her.'

'Unless there's a fire,' Claire reminded her friend.

'Or an earthquake,' Hailey said grudgingly.

'You'd have to,' Claire said. 'You'd have no choice.'

'But I'd never call her on the phone with our code.'

'No. You never would.'

Sometimes it was a comfort to say the thing you were most afraid of aloud. Tonight, Claire felt certain that stars would shine as brightly, no matter where a person was when she watched them. Even if someone was at the bottom of the deepest sea, the light would find her.

When it was nearly nine o'clock, the girls went to retrieve Aquamarine. Silvery moonlight was spilling into the cafeteria. Raymond looked a little stunned when the girls said he'd better say good-bye to their cousin. Time had a habit of moving too fast. Anyone could see that from the expression on Raymond's face.

'Already?' he said mournfully. All last night he had dreamed of the ocean, and now it seemed to him that he might be dreaming still.

'It's not time,' Aquamarine insisted. 'It can't be over.'

But it was. Beneath the wheelchair a circle of fish scales the color of moonlight had collected. Each one was now evaporating into fine, green dust.

'Can I have your phone number?' Raymond asked the mermaid as the girls hurried to wheel her out the door. 'Your address?'

'No,' Hailey and Claire said at the same time. 'She's going away.'

71

'I'm going away, too,' Raymond said, confused.

'Well, she's going farther,' Claire told him.

'She's going someplace you can't ever get to,' Hailey added.

But Aquamarine knew better. She unhooked one of the shells from her beautiful blue dress and gave it to Raymond. She promised that if he said her name into the shell, she would hear him, no matter where she might be.

'I don't think that's possible.' Raymond shook his head. He'd read so many books that he thought he knew how every story ended.

'Anything is possible,' Aquamarine told

him, and when the girls looked at her face, they knew that this was true.

Aquamarine didn't say a word when the girls brought her back to the pool. If she was crying, she didn't let them see. Tomorrow at noon, high tide would race in. Aquamarine was sure of this because a mermaid can always tell the tide, just as easily as a person can distinguish night from day. It was then she'd have to leave.

The girls stored the wheelchair in an abandoned cabana and promised they'd be back in the morning, first thing. Aquamarine had become so weak from her stay on land she hadn't any strength left. She was too exhausted to swim and was forced to stay in the shallow end of the pool. All the same, she refused to take off the blue dress, even though it weighed her down. By now, Aquamarine was as pale as those fish you find beached on the shore, and she'd begun to labour for breath.

'This is the most beautiful night there has ever been,' the mermaid whispered.

The girls ran to the parking lot where Maury was dozing behind the wheel of his car.

'So,' he asked when they got in the car. 'Was your mermaid happy with tonight's results?'

'She said it was the most beautiful night there had ever been,' Claire said.

74

Aquamarine

When the girls looked around them, they saw that this was true. Hailey and Claire peered back through the Capri gates, to the beach where the white crests of the waves broke on the shore. They could see the stars sparkling above. To have a night like this could make almost anyone believe in the future.

The furniture in Claire's grandparents' house was gone now, and because of this they were all supposed to sleep at Hailey's. But the girls begged and pleaded and at last the grown-ups gave in and allowed them to take their sleeping bags and camp out in the empty living room at Claire's house. It felt funny to be there without the sofa and the table and the pillows and the books and everything else that had made this Claire's home. Their voices echoed off the bare walls.

'Do you think she'll really go tomorrow?' Hailey asked.

'She has to,' Claire said. 'She doesn't have a choice.'

'Well, I wish she could stay.' Hailey's voice sounded strange, as though she were about to cry, but of course it was Claire who had always been the crier, not Hailey. Or at least this had been true up until now.

'You know what?' Right then Claire felt

Aquamarine

certain that some things really did stay the same. 'I think she wishes that, too.'

CHAPTER FIVE

On Saturday, the owner of the Capri Beach
Club returned, along with his wife, his
children, his grandchildren, all his uncles
and aunts, and everyone who had ever
worked at the Capri. A good-bye party was
being held, with live music and a barbecue
and more people than the beach club had

seen all summer long. The line at the snack bar crisscrossed the patio, with crowds calling for sandwiches and sodas.

Streamers and balloons had been strung over the entranceway. Even the bulldozers had been decorated. But despite the crepe paper necklaces and the headdresses of streamers, the machines looked like yellow monsters. No one could disguise that their purpose was to dismantle the club.

'Where have all these people been all summer?' Hailey grumbled when she and Claire arrived. The girls made their way through the crowd. 'The one day we want some privacy, this place is mobbed.'

They spied Raymond, who had already

82

packed up his books and was leaving for Florida later that day. He was working hard, trying to keep up with the demand of the crowd, but when he noticed the girls, he left everything and came over. He had the white shell Aquamarine had given him on a chain around his neck. He looked as though he hadn't had a wink of sleep.

'How can I leave without saying good-bye to her?' he said to the girls.

'You'll just have to,' Hailey said.

'We all have to do what we don't want to do sometimes,' Claire added.

The girls looked nervously at the pool. At least the warning ropes were still up and none of the crowd had yet ventured near.

'Is there something you're not telling me?' Raymond asked.

One little boy was approaching the deep end. He had a fishing net in his hands and a look on his face that spelled trouble.

'Fishy,' the little boy said.

'If there's something we're not telling you, we're not telling you for your own good,' Claire said. 'And for Aquamarine's good, too.'

The little boy was standing at the very edge of the pool, teetering on the cement.

'Oh, no!' Hailey said.

'Get back here!' Claire cried.

But the little boy didn't listen, and as they watched, he fell with barely a splash

84

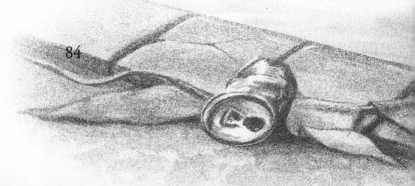

into the murky water. When Raymond saw what had happened, he ran so fast the girls could hardly keep up. He dove into the pool with his clothes and his shoes on. The girls could hear the little boy's parents calling to find their dear Arthur who was always such a wanderer.

His parents had no idea that Arthur had already been saved, and was secure in Raymond's and Aquamarine's arms. Someone else might have been shocked to see the silvery tail which guided Aquamarine through the water, but if anything, Raymond's eyes shone even brighter when he looked at her. As for the mermaid, she had used her last bit of strength to catch the boy when he fell. She was now as pale as moonlight, and so weak Raymond had to help her back to the shallow end of the pool. Thankfully, Arthur was so surprised to find that the fish he'd discovered was a girl that he didn't say a word.

'We have to take her back now,' Hailey said. 'We can't wait another minute!'

Raymond and Aquamarine looked at each other. Neither one wanted the other to leave, but without the ocean Aquamarine would fade into dust. By now, everyone was searching for Arthur and the crowd was coming dangerously close.

'Go on,' Raymond told the girls. 'I'll take care of things here.'

86

Aquamarine

Aquamarine turned to him then. Her voice was light as sea mist. 'Wherever you are,' she said. 'I'll find you.'

While the girls carried Aquamarine out of the pool to place her in the wheelchair she whispered something that sounded like *thank you*. She had become so dehydrated from her time on land that she was now surprisingly light and all that was left of her voice was a trickle.

Raymond went to the far end of the pool and waved his arms in the air. 'Over here,' he called to the crowd. He had wrapped Arthur in a blanket and now he lifted the boy up for all to see. Everyone turned to look, and in that moment the girls slipped away with Aquamarine.

The crowd surged around the rescued Arthur. People cheered and called Raymond a hero, and not one of them noticed that Raymond was paying no attention to their acclaim. He was looking to make sure the girls were on their way to the sea, wishing only that Aquamarine would be safe.

Hailey and Claire were already racing the wheelchair past the tennis courts where the weeds were as tall as trees, past the cabanas that hadn't been used all summer long, past the snack bar where Raymond would never work again. The owner of the beach club spied them, and he yelled for them to stay off the beach, but they went on anyway, past

the bulldozers, until the sand was too deep to roll the wheelchair along. They had reached the sea wall, made of cement and stones, which stood four feet tall.

'We have to carry her over,' Hailey said.

By now, the mermaid was light as air, dusty and dry as the sand. The girls made a seat for her out of their crossed arms and Aquamarine held on to their shoulders. Together, they made their way over the cement wall, then jumped down into the water. It was high tide and the surf was rough, but it was the time when the mermaid had to go. They could hear the owner yelling at them, but his words were lost in the crashing noise at the shore.

'We're going to have to bring her all the way in, past the breaking waves,' Claire said.

Hailey looked at her friend who had always been so afraid of water and felt immensely proud of her.

Together they carried Aquamarine. Her long hair blew out behind her and her skin gave off puffs of greenish dust, as if she were already turning to ash, right there in their arms.

'Hurry,' Claire shouted over the sound of the surf. 'We're losing her.'

They went in past the whitecaps that shone like stars, past the water that was wilder than horses. Over the crashing they could hear the sound of the mermaid's six

90

sisters singing to her, urging her to quickly return to where she belonged.

Aquamarine seemed too weak to swim. At first, she was so limp she could not lift her head, but the farther into the water they brought her, the more she revived. Soon she splashed her tail, and before long she began to shimmer again, and when she laughed her watery laugh, they could tell it was time to let go. By then, the girls were up to their necks in the surf, doing their best to stay afloat in the rolling waves.

'We'll never forget you,' the girls told her, and at the very same moment, they opened their arms. Before they could blink, she was gone, deep into the waves, to the very bottom of the sea where her sisters were waiting to rejoice and take her home and keep her safe all the rest of her days.

By the time the girls helped each other back to shore, their arms and legs were aching, but they didn't want to let go of one another. They had both swallowed quarts of saltwater. They pulled strands of seaweed from their hair as they watched the sea, but all they could see were the waves. Aquamarine had disappeared without a trace. The girls might have felt as though they'd imagined her completely if they hadn't found the two white shells Aquamarine had left for them on the seat of the wheelchair. They were beautiful shells,

as white as the surf in the sea. When you held one up to your ear you could hear the sound of your best friend talking to you, even if she was a thousand miles away.

'What did I tell you girls!' the owner of the Capri shouted when Hailey and Claire waved to Raymond as he headed for the parking lot and roared off on his motorbike. 'Stay off the beach!'

'We just wanted to say good-bye,' they told him. And then they hugged the startled owner and thanked him for the best summer of their lives.

That evening, while dusk was spreading across the sky, Claire's grandparents loaded

93

up their car. The moving men had taken most of their belongings, but Claire had set aside anything that was irreplaceable. These items would be taken along on the ride down to Florida, to ensure they wouldn't get lost. There was the pearl necklace that had belonged to Claire's mother, and the photograph albums, and one of the white shells left by Aquamarine.

Hailey's mum had made up a picnic basket, with deviled eggs and chocolate cupcakes and a Thermos of pink lemonade, and she'd thrown in the necessities for anyone who leaves home: a compass, a map, and a photograph of the house that was left behind.

'It's all right if you talk to the girl who moves in here,' Claire told Hailey as her grandparents were buckling their seat belts and waving good-bye. 'I've thought it over, and I really want you to.'

'I might say hello or something. Just to be polite.'

'Even if there isn't a fire,' they both said at the very same time, the way they were still known to do.

Hailey and Claire hugged each other right there on the lawn that Claire's grandfather had cared for so meticulously. It was still the best lawn in the neighbourhood, and Hailey would be around to make certain the new people watered early in the morning, which was always best for any garden.

Hailey stood where she was and waved until Claire's grandparents' car disappeared. After that, she stood there a while longer. It was still August, but it didn't feel like summer anymore. All of a sudden the crickets' call was faster, as if they knew that in only a week school would begin. It was obvious, even to the insects, that it would be quite some time before the weather turned hot again.

That night, Hailey's mum fixed rainbow sundaes, which had always been Claire and Hailey's favorite treat. Vanilla ice cream, strawberries, blueberries, hot fudge, and

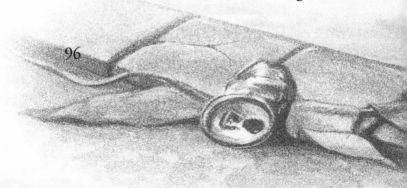

Aquamarine

butterscotch. But Hailey couldn't eat. She went to the kitchen window even though it wasn't possible to see anything next door. Just an empty house, without any curtains, or any people, or anything at all. Hailey got out her white seashell and she held it to her ear. The whooshing sound within was exactly like Claire's voice, and Hailey hoped that if she spoke into the shell Claire would hear her, no matter how far away she already was. *Safe trip*, that's what she called to her friend. *Here's to the future*, she said.

CHAPTER SIX

On the day the bulldozers knocked down the Capri Beach Club, the weather changed at last. The sky was as grey as fish scales and the air was salty and wet. Hailey and her mum stood in the parking lot to watch. Before long, the entranceway was crushed, the patio was levelled, and the fence around the pool was shoved aside. Hundreds of seagulls and terns circled in the sky.

The pool had already been drained, and in no time the bulldozers set to work breaking down the concrete. It was hard to tell which was noisier, the sound of the machines at work or the rumble of the wild surf.

Hailey had brought her camera along, and she'd planned to take a photograph to send to Claire so that she could see what had happened to the Capri, but it didn't even seem like the same place any more.

'I think it's better if she just remembers it the way it was,' Hailey told her mother.

True enough, some things were best

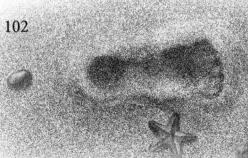

kept as a memory, but some things changed for the better. Claire, for instance, had taken up swimming, which only made sense since she now lived right on the beach. As it turned out, she was good at it. She took to the water if not like a mermaid, then at least like a fish.

Of course, if she hadn't started swimming, she would have never run into Raymond, who was on his college team and often practised in the blue bay that Claire could see from her window. The first time she spotted him, Claire thought Raymond was a seal, that's how far out in the water he was, but then he waved to her and swam over.

'I never thanked you and your friend for introducing me to Aquamarine,' Raymond said.

'I'm sorry it didn't work out,' Claire said.

'But it did.' Raymond was surprised. 'She said she would find me, and she did.'

When he swam back into the sea, Claire could see that he wasn't really alone. There in the deepest blue water was a girl who was waiting for him, far beyond the breaking waves. For some time afterward, Claire brought her camera down to the beach, hoping for a photograph of Aquamarine to send to Hailey. But after a while she put her camera away. Hailey would be coming to visit next summer and that wasn't so very far

Aquamarine

away. If they were lucky, if they watched carefully, they might still be able to spy Aquamarine. Far beyond the tide pools and the jellyfish, beyond starfish and snails, she is swimming there still.

Indigo

CHAPTER ONE

The town of Oak Grove was so far away from the ocean that most people who lived there had never seen a seagull or listened to the whisper of a pink shell. They certainly hadn't heard the way the sea can call to you on a hot July day when wave after wave beckons and the water is endless and clear.

As a matter of fact, people in Oak Grove dreaded water. This was a town with a history of terrible flooding. Fifteen years earlier, the spring that fed Penman's Creek overflowed, leaving Oak Grove awash so that people had to clamber onto their roofs. When the floodwaters finally receded, the creek was dammed up, and folks went overboard to protect Oak Grove. The town council ordered the public swimming pool drained; lawn watering was limited to an hour a day, showers to ten minutes long. Drier was better in Oak Grove, or so people said. And the weather appeared to cooperate. The only thing that seemed endless here was the perfect blue sky that was the same day after day, without the slightest hint of rain or the hope of a stray cloud passing by.

Most residents of Oak Grove were grateful for its climate. But not Martha Glimmer. As far as Martha was concerned, this was the worst year of her life. Martha hated Oak Grove, where there was nothing better to do on a brilliant spring day than sit on the roof of her father's garage with her two best friends, Trevor and Eli McGill, and throw rocks at the line of tin cans they'd arranged down below.

Martha hated the fact that it never rained in Oak Grove; she hated the way the grass grew so dry, it creaked when you walked on it; and she hated Hildy Swoon, a neighbour who brought casseroles over almost every night and tried to convince Martha's father that he should start a new life. Most of all, Martha hated people who pitied a girl like herself, who'd lost her mother the year before, at such a tender age. While Martha was at it, she hated being thirteen, a number that was clearly unlucky, at least for her, for this was the year when she'd grown seven inches; her legs were now so long and gawky, she often tripped over her own feet.

Martha's friend, Trevor McGill, completely disagreed; he enjoyed being thirteen. He had grown taller as well, one of the few boys their age who was the same

4

Indigo

height as Martha. But whereas Martha was uncomfortable with her size, Trevor couldn't be happier with his. As for Trevor's brother, Eli, at eleven, he was at an age when anything older was preferable, and could hardly wait to grow up.

Both the McGill brothers had dark hair and sea-green eyes, and they certainly weren't like anyone else in town. It wasn't anything obvious that set the boys apart, but when you considered some of their odder traits, the little things added up. From the time the boys were toddlers there had been gossip about them. Susie Lawrence, who worked at the Sweet Shoppe, confided that the boys threw away any candy their mother bought them, tossing out jelly beans and chocolate bars alike, and that wasn't very normal, was it? Their old baby-sitter, Gretchen Hardy, whispered that Trevor and Eli had refused to nap unless she brought them into the kitchen. They'd cry and bellow like walruses until Gretchen turned on the tap full blast, and then, instantly, the sound of running water lulled them to sleep.

As the boys grew older, they grew stranger as well, or so people said, especially those folks who enjoyed gossip far more than they enjoyed their neighbours' good fortune. But who could blame people for discussing how odd it was that Eli McGill had been found splashing around in a

6

bathtub – thankfully, with all his clothes on – at Annamaria Chamberlain's tenth birthday party while everyone else devoured cake and ice cream. Or how unnerving it was when Trevor fixed people with his pale green eyes, staring until even the most landlocked citizens found themselves dreaming of running off to sea with the wind at their backs and everything else in their lives just a memory.

Most of Oak Grove had noticed that the brothers seemed to live on a diet of fish, preferring tuna and sardines to pizza and burgers. Those who were closest to the boys' parents, Charlie and Kate McGill, admitted they'd been startled to see Trevor and Eli add handfuls of salt to their drinking water and then swallow it down without a burp, as if the briny mixture had come from a clear mountain spring.

And so it was understandable that people in Oak Grove were wary of the McGill boys, but in the most polite and orderly way. This was a town where everything was orderly, after all, another thing Martha Glimmer hated about it. Streets crisscrossed at perfect right angles; houses had to be painted white by decree of the town council; children went to the same school their parents had attended, and were as predictable and reliable as their forefathers, the ones who'd taught their sons and daughters to follow the rules instead of their hearts.

It was following his heart that had led Eli McGill to free the frogs in the science lab, even though the science teacher chased him all the way to the dried-out creek bed. But Eli was so fast, he couldn't be caught. The children of Oak Grove called him 'Eel' after that, and they dubbed his brother 'Trout', because of the older boy's green eyes that never seemed to blink and the gasping look he had whenever someone was being bullied in the school yard, as if someone else's pain caused him heartache as well.

Perhaps these nicknames stuck because of the characteristic most people considered strangest of all about the brothers. Although it had never bothered Martha Glimmer one bit, most folks in town found something else about Trout and Eel particularly alarming: the boys had a thin webbing between their fingers and toes.

Dr Marsh, who'd been Oak Grove's physician for a good thirty years and who was rarely flustered, blinked when the young McGill boys were brought in for their first visit after they'd been adopted. When he saw the webbing he gulped like a fish himself and admitted he'd never seen anything like it before. But they were good, healthy boys, and Dr Marsh patted their sleek heads and told Kate and Charlie McGill that, given all the things that could go wrong in this world,

10

a meshing of skin between a child's fingers and toes was nothing to worry about. In time, it would probably wear away.

But now that the boys were thirteen and eleven it was clear the trait was permanent, and although this made certain activities difficult – a proper baseball mitt was impossible to find, and bowling was out of the question – Eel's fingers could spread so wide, he could play a duet on the piano all by himself, and Trout could palm a basketball with no trouble at all.

The brothers' unusual taste in food never diminished, but that was easily accommodated as well. When Jeanette Morton, who owned the bakery, realised the boys preferred anchovy pies to chocolate cakes, she happily perfected a crust so flaky, and a filling so rich, that even Mr McGill, who'd always loved sweets, grew to prefer anchovy pie to apple or blueberry. Martha's father, who owned the grocery, ordered fresh tuna each week, which Mrs McGill served raw for the boys and lightly broiled for herself and her husband. As for all the salt the brothers consumed, well, their mother told people such a preference was probably caused by a vitamin deficiency.

By now Martha Glimmer barely noticed anything unusual about her two friends. Some people say 'live and let live', and that was the group Martha belonged to. A real

Indigo

friend believes in you when you don't believe in yourself, and this had always been true for Martha and the boys, especially when Martha's mother fell ill. But there will always be those who zero in on anything different and turn such habits and traits into ammunition – Richard Grady, for instance, their classmate who called Trout 'flipper boy' and asked Eel right to his face how it felt to look like a water snake.

Martha Glimmer wasn't interested in the opinions of Richard Grady or of anyone else in Oak Grove. She wasn't planning on staying in this boring town one second longer than necessary. She wanted to go to New York and San Francisco and Paris, cities where her mother had lived before she'd come to Oak Grove and married Martha's father, before she opened the dancing school over on Main Street, right above the bakery, where the aroma of chocolate and vanilla bean wafted up through the ceiling, so that children who took lessons there always seemed sweeter following an hour of stretches and pliés or an afternoon spent learning the rudiments of the tango.

After Martha's mother had passed on last year, Hildy Swoon began bringing over her casseroles. She fixed terrible tasting concoctions made out of rice and peas, canned soup and potatoes, but Martha's father was so heartbroken, he didn't seem to notice how awful the food was.

From the start, Hildy Swoon made it clear that she wasn't interested in Martha's company. When she stayed for dinner, Hildy informed Martha that she preferred children to eat in the kitchen rather than the dining room to ensure that the adults wouldn't be disturbed. Although Mr Glimmer seemed grateful for the help around the house, he didn't notice that Hildy didn't seem to like much about Martha, and she certainly didn't like the McGill brothers. Whenever she was visiting and the boys came to call, Hildy made a clicking, disapproving sound, like a hen that can't get comfortable on her nest.

'Those boys are much too strange,' Hildy

told Martha and her father. 'There is definitely something fishy about them.'

In Martha's opinion some people were meant to be mothers, and some people, such as Hildy Swoon, were not. You could easily tell who was who by whether or not they listened to you. Hildy Swoon always hummed when Martha spoke and then she said, 'What?' when it was perfectly clear she hadn't listened to a word and couldn't care less about what Martha thought. Kate McGill, on the other hand, was clearly meant to be somebody's mother. She stopped what she was doing whenever her boys came rushing into the house. One look and anyone could tell her happiness could

16

be measured in direct proportion to the happiness of her sons.

Each spring, Mrs McGill celebrated the anniversary of the day when she and her husband had adopted the boys. Charlie McGill had closed down his construction company and they'd gone on vacation to Ocean City, expecting to bring home nothing more than seashells and sand in their shoes. Instead, they'd returned to Oak Grove with the two boys, and from then on Kate McGill had been the happiest woman in town.

Martha Glimmer felt welcome at the McGills' night or day. There were always plates of seaweed cakes, which tasted far better than they sounded, and fish soup simmering on the stove. At the Glimmers' the only place Martha and her friends felt comfortable was up on the roof of the garage now that Hildy was so often around, mopping the floors with ammonia and straightening out the dresser drawers. The friends spent most afternoons with nothing better to do but knock down the cans they had placed in a line down below in the grass.

'You are so lucky,' Martha told Trout and Eel. 'You have such a great family.'

Her own father had gotten sadder with each day of Martha's mother's illness. By the time Hildy started to call, he didn't seem like

18

himself any more. The man he used to be would have never let Hildy Swoon take over their house. He would have never been too grief-stricken to notice that his daughter left the room every time Hildy walked in.

'Lucky?' Trout held up a webbed hand.

'That's nothing,' Martha insisted. 'That's not the only thing people should see when they look at you.'

Trout had no idea how handsome he was. He didn't care about such things. He concentrated on knocking down more cans than his brother did before giving Martha her turn. One day, Martha might be a dancer in New York City or Paris and Trout might fall in love with her, but for now they were both thirteen and she beat him and Eel at their game, knocking down ten cans in a row.

'Now, that's luck,' Trout teased.

Martha made a face at him, but she knew that Trout was always glad when she won. This was one more reason why she didn't care if he was different. What mattered was that Trout McGill was the one person aside from her mother who believed that Martha would some day leave Oak Grove, and that no matter how tall she was, or how uncomfortable with herself, she would be a dancer. He believed in dreams, in the endings that people told you could never happen, in disappointments reversed and luck that lasted.

Indigo

Perhaps this was because Trout's own dream was a simple one. He wanted to see the ocean.

Trout was the sort of person who could be talking to you and daydreaming at the same time and you wouldn't even know it, except that every now and then he'd murmur tide or starfish when a simple yes or no would have done. Again and again he'd asked his parents to take him to the shore, but each time he had, Kate McGill had gotten a worried look and Charlie McGill would start planning a vacation that would take them hiking high up into the mountains.

'You used to go to Ocean City every year. I've seen the photographs,' Trout would say.

'I'm thirteen and I've never even been to the beach.'

'I'm eleven and I've never collected sea-shells,' Eel would add, although he had a conch shell, which he'd taken from the science lab, that he kept hidden under his bed. When he held the shell to his ear the lullaby of the waves inside helped him fall asleep.

One weekend Trout and Eel decided to paint their bedroom blue. The walls were the turquoise of the southern seas, the ceiling was cobalt, the floors indigo, the colour of waters so deep and distant, no human had ever seen them before. Here in this room anyone could imagine the sound

22

of waves breaking. Even Martha swore she could hear seagulls and smell the salt air.

It was a wonderful room, but Charlie McGill was not pleased when he opened the door and saw all that endless blue.

'If you knew what the ocean was like, you'd be grateful to live in a place as dry as Oak Grove,' Charlie told his boys. 'Water is dangerous, and that's always been true. Before the town ordered Penman's Creek drained and hired me to build the flood wall, we had a terrible time whenever a storm came through. People lost everything. Be glad you're here in Oak Grove, high and dry.'

A few days later, when the boys got home

from school, they found their room had been painted white. Gone were the southern seas and the farthest waters. Even Eel's seashell had disappeared, and he wondered how he would ever manage to get to sleep.

When Kate McGill saw the hurt expressions on the boys' faces, she tried to explain. 'You have to understand your father lived through the worst flood in Oak Grove's history. And then he had a terrible experience one year when we were on vacation in Ocean City. He tried to rescue someone from drowning, but it was too late. Ever since, he's been hydrophobic.'

Trout looked up *hydrophobia* in the dictionary. Charlie McGill was a kind and

24

generous man, but he was definitely hydrophobic – which was defined as a fear of water. As a matter of fact, Charlie's construction company specialised in tearing out bathtubs and replacing them with shower stalls. The less water the better, as far as he was concerned. Everyone knew Charlie would have worked for free building the wall of rocks that dammed up Penman's Creek if the town hadn't hired him for the job. Of course a man like that could not abide a room that was as blue as the sea.

'I can't believe your father did this,' Martha said when she saw the white room. She knew how much work the brothers had put into all that blue, and it wasn't fair for

25

the room to be returned to the way it had been before their effort. It wasn't right to have someone charge into your world without even asking, acting as if you were nothing more than an egg to be flipped and flopped, sunny-side up or scrambled, depending on the whims of whoever ran your life.

Hildy Swoon, for instance, had let herself into the Glimmers' house one day when no one was home. She had taken all of Martha's mother's clothes from the hall closet, packed them in boxes, and stored them in the attic without even asking. Martha had gone upstairs and retrieved her mother's yellow shawl, the one with the fringe and the embroidered poppies that made Martha feel as though she could travel through time whenever it was wrapped around her shoulders. Martha rarely danced any more, except when she wore the shawl. Then she could close her eyes and imagine she was back at the dance studio, which was now used as the bakery's storeroom. She could smell sugar and hear her mother's voice. She could dance like an angel, even though she was much too tall.

It was not long after the boys' room was repainted that Martha came home to find the shawl missing. She looked through her bureau, through her closet, even under her bed, but there was no mistake about it, the shawl was gone. Martha ran to the basement and there it was, hanging on a clothes line, shrunken and discoloured. Hildy came up behind her.

'I decided to wash that dirty old thing,' Hildy Swoon informed Martha. 'But it wasn't very well made.'

'It was silk.' Martha did her best not to let Hildy see her cry. 'It wasn't supposed to be washed like a rag.'

'Well, that's what it is now,' Hildy replied. 'But at least it's clean.'

Martha took the shawl, folded it carefully, and put it into her backpack, where it would be safe from Hildy. That evening she went over to the McGills', where

she found the boys sitting on the roof of their own garage since they no longer felt comfortable in their white room. Martha climbed up the ladder and sat in between the brothers. Together they dreamed of starting new lives. They'd live by the ocean, they'd visit New York City, they'd paint every room in their house blue, then swim and dance beneath the constellations each night.

'But we're trapped here,' Martha moaned.

'High and dry,' Trout said moodily, his eyes flashing the colour of the sea during a storm.

'Not necessarily,' Eel said.

Eel didn't believe anything should be trapped, not frogs, not fish, and certainly not people. He was fearless and smart and he didn't speak much, unless he had something worth saying. At such times, Eel would speak his mind no matter the consequences.

'There's nobody who could stop us if we decided to leave. It's the only way we'll ever get to see the ocean,' Eel declared.

Martha and Trout looked at each other. The lilacs were blooming as best they could in a town that was so dry, even the stars looked dusty up in the sky. Eel's idea passed between Martha and Trout like a blue wave. Sometimes words spoken are the ones you've been afraid to think, but once they're said aloud there's no way to make them disappear. There, on a clear evening, in a town where it

Indigo

seemed nothing ever happened and nothing ever changed, these three friends decided to take hold of their fate.

CHAPTER TWO

At midnight the wind in the trees can sound like the ocean. The moonlight can make a road appear as endless as the sea. Martha noticed this as she climbed out of her window, stopping to tack a note for her father on the door before she headed to meet the McGills. She had her backpack, in which she had stowed crackers and peanut butter for herself, sardines for the boys, along with a change of clothes and her mother's yellow shawl.

Being out so late reminded Martha of the way her mother sometimes would wake her unexpectedly to bring her out onto the lawn to dance beneath the stars. Standing in the dark and thinking about her mother and the way she would laugh as they sneaked out of the house, as if they shared the best secret in the world, did something strange to Martha. Her mother suddenly seemed present in some deep way. Martha didn't know if she could take another step. But then she heard Trout whistle, and she started running.

Indigo

Before she knew it, she was halfway down the road, to the place where Trout and Eel were waiting beside the mailbox that Hildy Swoon had cleaned with a stiff metal brush to get rid of every bit of dust and grime.

'We have a compass and thirty-five dollars,' Eel told Martha as they started down the road. 'We charted the route to Ocean City, and if we walk eight hours a day we'll be there in ten days.'

'Ten days?' Martha was surprised. 'I only brought enough food for one night.'

'You don't have to go.' Trout didn't look at Martha as he spoke. She knew he was giving her the chance to change her mind.

'Of course I do.' Martha wasn't about to

37

lose her best friends. If they were gone, there would be no one to talk to. No one to trust. 'You'd be lost without me,' she said.

People went searching for their dreams all the time, didn't they? Still, Martha dragged behind the boys in the moonlight. She was thinking about how sad her father was and how he would feel when he went to wake her for school and discovered she was gone. All he would find was her open window, along with the note on the door. *I'm sorry*, she'd written. *I love you, but I don't feel I belong here any more.*

'Race you to the town line,' Eel called.

The friends ran as fast as they could, with Eel, always the fastest, out in front. They raced down Main Street, past the shuttered grocery that Martha's father owned, past the bakery and what was once the dance studio, past Charlie McGill's construction company. They turned onto Elm and ran along the dried-out bed of Penman's Creek. They hurried through the dark, raising clouds of dust, laughing until they reached the sign that said OAK GROVE. HOME SWEET HOME.

Martha stared at the words. Her throat and eyes felt hot, as if this silly sign could make her cry.

'Which way?' Eel said softly in the dark.

The moon was behind a cloud, and Martha and Trout felt tentative as well. They were both thinking of people who'd

disappeared and were never found again, and of how hard it was to leave behind the people you loved, even if the life you wanted wasn't the one they could give you.

Trout took out the compass, then pointed down the road. 'East to the ocean. We just keep going.'

They told themselves they weren't runaways, they were run-tos. But running is running either way. After a while, they all felt as though they had eaten spoonfuls of lead, and that made running even more difficult. After the first mile they had the shivers. A mile more and they had the shakes. Oak Grove seemed very far away, and when they walked through the woods they could hear things moving. Owls and shrews, foxes and rabbits. Deer so startled to see the three friends cutting across the meadows, they froze in place.

When Martha's feet began to hurt and the boys' eyes grew blurry, they stopped to make camp beneath a twisted oak tree, one of the oldest in the county. Tomorrow, school would start at exactly eight-thirty, but they wouldn't be in attendance. If they hadn't had other concerns they might have begun to worry about what people would think when they didn't show up for their classes, but for now, all they could concentrate on was their growling stomachs. Martha unpacked the food she had brought along, and Eel produced a Thermos, although too much salt had been added to the water for Martha to take more than a sip.

In the moonlight the McGill brothers' complexions turned faintly blue, and the webbing between their fingers was iridescent.

'What's the matter?' Trout asked when he caught Martha staring. 'Afraid you're out here with freaks?'

'I'm out here with my two best friends,' Martha said.

Trout looked at her with so much gratitude, Martha knew they would be friends forever, no matter what their final destination might be.

Eel was exhausted, but ever since he'd

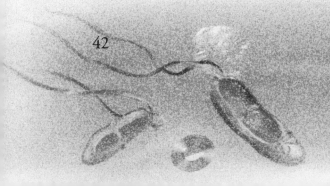

lost his seashell he'd had trouble getting to sleep. He needed a story, the comforting babble of voices like waves on the shore. 'Tell me about when you danced with your mother,' he said to Martha.

'We'd go outside when everyone else in town was sleeping,' Martha told him, even though she'd told him this story many times before. 'She always wore her yellow shawl.'

Martha reached into her backpack and brought out the shrunken shawl, and the boys understood that even though she was running to something, she was also running away.

'You can still wear it,' Trout told her. 'You can dance right here. Right now.'

But there were no stars in the sky, and Martha shook her head. Her face was cloudy. 'I don't know if I remember the dances. I'm afraid that before long I won't remember her, either.'

'We don't remember our first mother,' Eel said. The boys rarely spoke of their lives before they'd come to Oak Grove.

'I remember,' Trout said. 'Or at least, some things. I remember that she liked to swim, and when she laughed it sounded like a waterfall.'

They were so tired, they fell asleep without trying. They were still far from the ocean, but Trout dreamed the same dream he had every night. He was on a beach, and

44

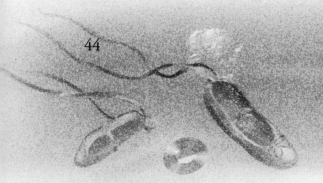

before him the water was dark. A storm was coming up, just like Charlie McGill always feared, and out in the waves, someone was hurt and going under. Someone was calling to him. *Swim,* she was saying. *Swim to the land.*

Where Eel slept, in a tangle of leaves, he had the very same dream as his brother, but he didn't know it. Because he was younger he didn't remember as much, awake or in his dreams. All he saw were the blue waves. Whoever was calling was so far out to sea, he couldn't make out her face. The blue of everything was filling up his eyes, and his heart, and everything he had ever known.

Martha had a different dream entirely. In

her dream she was on a street that was made of sugar, and every time she tried to dance, she slipped and there was no one beside her to break her fall. Martha lurched out of sleep, still feeling as though she were falling. It was morning, but the sky was grey and thick with storm clouds. This was definitely not good weather for running to anything. Up above, the branches of the old oak were shaking, harder and harder still. One of the branches groaned as it broke. Before Martha could move away, it crashed onto her arm.

Without thinking, she called out for her mother. Trout hurried over and hauled the branch off. He asked Martha if she could move her arm, but it hurt too much to try.

46

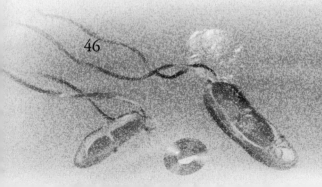

Indigo

'This isn't good,' Trout said.

'It will be fine,' Martha insisted, but she didn't sound very sure of herself, and when she sat up the pain made her gasp. She could tell from the expression in Trout's eyes that the dream of the ocean was fading, and she didn't want to be the reason for a loss like that. 'I mean it will be fine,' she insisted. 'And I'm not going back, if that's what you're thinking.'

'You have to see Dr Marsh,' Trout told her. 'I'm pretty certain it's broken.'

The wind was so wild, they had to shout just to hear each other.

'This isn't your fault,' Trout hollered. 'We just picked the wrong day to leave.

I've never seen weather like this.'

True enough, Oak Grove hadn't had more than morning dew for years, and now the sky was swirling and Martha's arm was throbbing. All the same, even if she had to go back, she didn't have to ruin everything. 'You should go on without me.'

'Maybe I should,' Trout said. 'I just don't want to.'

When Martha heard this, she smiled in spite of the pain she felt. Trout McGill would never abandon his best friend. For the first time in ages, Martha felt happy, even though her arm ached.

They woke Eel, who lurched to his feet, arms flailing, as though he'd been drowning in his sleep. When they explained they had to turn back, Eel didn't argue, and a part of him, the part that was worried about Charlie and Kate McGills' hearts being broken when they opened the brothers' bedroom door and found them gone, was relieved.

The weather was more threatening by the minute. Rabbits ran into the hollows. Blackbirds tried to hide in the thickets. Thunder echoed and came closer. Soon enough, the first big drops began to fall. It was the sort of rain that was cold and nasty and fell in sheets, as though a spigot had been turned on up in the sky. Martha was chilled to the bone. The boys, however, weren't bothered in the least by the rain.

They drank in the drops and laughed as their clothes and shoes became soaked. Watching them, Martha felt she had never seen her friends happier. It was as if they'd been desperate for water all their lives.

In town, people woke up in fear, remembering the storm of the past. The wind had already blown away the note Martha had left for her father and torn the paper into tatters. That same wind whipped through one room after another as Kate and Charlie McGill searched for their sons. The bakery shut down for the first time in fifteen years, with a batch of cinnamon rolls still in the oven, for electricity and gas lines were knocked out by the strong gusts. Dogs

Indigo

huddled under tables and refused to go into their yards. Children stayed home from school. The sky looked the way an ocean does when a hurricane is near, with swells twenty feet tall, and wind mixing with water, and no mercy for those on land or at sea.

Martha and the McGill boys knew they had to hurry. The morning had turned as dark as night. The friends had never seen a sky so wild. Lightning split the horizon, and water poured down. When at last they reached the road, they saw that the gullies and ditches had filled and were beginning to overflow. Meadows were turning into lakes, and Penman's Creek

was a rushing river whose waters were unable to drain because of the stone wall.

At first the water on the road was up to the friends' ankles; then it was up to their knees. They couldn't help but think of the old days they'd heard about, when all of Oak Grove was submerged underwater and people lost everything they owned.

By now, the rain was so heavy, Martha could barely see where she was going.

'Just follow the white line down the middle of the road,' Trout shouted over the wind, but before long that line disappeared into the swirl of murky water that was quickly reaching their waists.

Eel took out his compass, and they tried

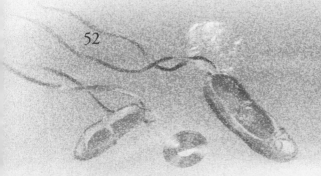

Indigo

their best to head west, huddled together to prevent the wind from buffeting Martha and her aching arm. Just when they thought they had journeyed in the wrong direction they came upon the sign – OAK GROVE. HOME SWEET HOME. Although it had all but vanished in the rising waters, the sign was still the highest, driest spot around. Martha took out her mother's shawl before she let the backpack float away. The three friends hurried to roost on the very top of the sign. From this perch they saw that all over Oak Grove people had climbed onto their rooftops and were clinging to their chimneys. Penman's Creek had overflowed, and the centre of town was the hardest hit.

53

'This is horrible,' Martha said, thinking of her father having to bail out their basement and the grocery store. She noticed the brothers were grinning. 'What is it?' she demanded. 'What's so funny?'

'It looks like the way we pictured the ocean,' Trout told her.

The rain had slowed to a mere pitter-patter, and they realised that what they heard now were the floodwaters washing back and forth like a tide.

'Listen,' Eel said. It was just like the echo inside his shell. One wave after another. Water as far as the eye could see.

CHAPTER THREE

By afternoon the sky had begun to turn blue, and the three friends had dried out on their perch above the sign. Trout had made a sling from Martha's mother's shawl to ensure that her arm would be protected from further harm until they got to Dr Marsh's.

'We're still just as far away from the

ocean as ever,' Martha said. 'There go your dreams.'

'I'm starting to think that my dream is real,' Trout said as he looked out over the water. 'I remember being in the ocean. I remember our mother tried to protect us when a speedboat came too close, and the propeller hit her.'

Trout might have recalled more if they hadn't heard somebody shouting. 'Save me!' a boy was screaming as he was dragged along what used to be downtown but what was now downstream. It was Richard Grady, who had so enjoyed calling the McGill brothers names. One minute Richard had been riding his bike, taunting the cats stuck up in trees and laughing at folks who were bailing out their basements, and the next minute Penman's Creek had overflowed and he'd been washed away. Like most of the children in this dry town he'd never learned how to swim. Now, Richard Grady held tight to his floating bicycle, thrashing and screaming, certain he was about to drown. 'Help me!' he called to the friends on their perch.

Before Martha could call back that Richard had better ask nicely if he wanted their help, and apologise for every nasty word he'd ever said, Trout jumped into the water, cutting through the currents as though he were indeed related to his namesake. He grabbed Richard by his sleeve before he was washed into even deeper waters, and Eel jumped in after his brother to help haul Richard to the safety of the Oak Grove sign. When Richard climbed up, the sign shook under his weight, and Martha had to hold on tight with her good arm.

'A thank-you would be in order,' Martha advised as Richard Grady wiped the water out of his eyes.

'Oh, yeah. Sure. Thanks.' Richard was still in shock by how quickly the world had shifted. Six feet of water where before there had been none, and those he least expected to save him becoming his rescuers.

'I hope you regret calling the McGills all

those horrid names,' Martha said.

'I don't know about that.' Richard peered into the water. 'I still don't think they're exactly normal. You may have noticed, they're not coming up for air.'

Martha saw that indeed Trout and Eel had disappeared in the murky water. The oddest things were floating by – flowerpots and trash cans, doghouses and mailboxes – but there wasn't a glimpse of the boys.

Martha grabbed Richard by the collar of his soaking shirt. 'Where did they go?' she demanded, her voice shaking.

'Under the water.' Richard seemed a little afraid of how upset Martha was. 'I swear they were there one minute and gone the next.'

Martha jumped down from the sign to find that the water was now much too deep to stand. She took a deep breath and went under, straining to keep her eyes open, frantically searching for her friends. She worried about what tragic and watery scene might greet her, but there the boys were, swimming underwater, having the time of their lives.

When they caught sight of Martha, they waved, but Martha couldn't wave back. She had lost her balance and been pulled into a whirlpool, a spinning circle of wild water right at the corner of Elm Street, where Penman's Creek ran into the gutters.

With only one strong arm, it was

Indigo

impossible for Martha to break free of the whirlpool. She felt herself going down, and she saw a bit of her life race before her eyes – her father's kind face, the yellow stars of a summer night, her mother's cool hands when Martha was little and suffering from a fever. Maybe these images helped her to think fast. Before she could be carried away, Martha pulled off the sling that had been made of her mother's shawl and lassoed one of the posts of the Oak Grove sign. The silk shawl was surprisingly strong; not even the whirlpool could take Martha away.

It took only a few seconds for the McGill boys to swim to Martha. One blink and they were there, helping her into calmer waters.

'Are you OK?' Trout asked.

Despite the pain in her arm and a tight feeling in her chest, Martha nodded. She had let go of the shawl when the McGill boys pulled her to safety, and it hung on the sign like a banner before the waters washed it away. Martha felt tears sting her eyes.

'Boy oh boy, I thought you were a goner,' Richard Grady called to Martha from his perch.

'Then why didn't you help?' Martha called back. As the McGill brothers guided Martha onto the only high ground left, a stretch that ran parallel to Main Street that had been a hill before the flood, Martha thought about how comfortable Trout and

Eel had seemed underwater. They'd looked as though they were somewhere they finally belonged.

From high on the hill the friends had an even better view of town. They could hear people shouting and calling for help. Even Richard Grady, now alone on the sign, was worried.

'My father said the water will keep rising until the wall at the creek is taken down,' he said. 'Then the water could flow out of town the way it used to.'

Trout and Eel looked at each other. Even though they knew it had taken Charlie McGill and his crew two weeks to build the wall, Martha could tell what the McGill

boys had in mind. She would have helped if she could, but it was clear she could never keep up with her friends, not even if she had the use of both of her arms.

'Good luck,' she cried as the boys dove into the water.

Someone was calling her name, and Martha looked to see Jeanette Morton from the bakery stuck on the other side of the hill. Jeanette was sitting on the roof of her car eating cinnamon rolls. Martha sloshed over, and Jeanette helped her up. Martha was so hungry, she ate two of the delicious pastries before she answered Jeanette's question of what had happened to her arm.

Indigo

'Possibly broken,' Martha said between mouthfuls.

'My goodness!' Jeanette said. 'And what do the McGill boys think they're doing? That water is dangerous.'

'They'll be fine,' Martha said, trying to convince herself of their safety as well. After all, she had seen how they swam underwater, their webbed hands flashing like flippers.

'What about your father? Is he all right?' Jeanette had an expression that was both worried and faraway. She had been a good friend of Martha's mother, but ever since Hildy had entered the picture, she hadn't come around.

'I'm sure Hildy's taking care of him,' Martha reminded her.

'Oh, Hildy,' Jeanette said sadly.

'Oak Grove is filled with awful things and terrible people,' Martha said. 'I'm like my mother when it comes to this town. I belong in a city, like New York or Paris or San Francisco. I'm leaving as soon as I can.'

'But your mother loved Oak Grove. She told me the happiest day of her life was when she came here and met your father. She used to go out in the field beyond Penman's Creek at night and dance before you were born.' Jeanette smiled at the memory. 'I went with her sometimes. I never saw anything as beautiful.'

Indigo

Before Martha had time to think this over, a rowboat appeared on the flooded road. There were her father and Charlie McGill, paddling down the centre of Main Street.

'Ahoy!' Jeanette Morton called, waving both hands above her head.

'Jeanette, you're a peach. You rescued my daughter,' Mr Glimmer called, and Martha didn't bother to correct her father. She didn't let him know she hadn't needed rescuing, because she saw the way Jeanette Morton was beaming. Martha couldn't help but wish that Jeanette had been the one who had started bringing over casseroles.

'Thank goodness you're safe,' Mr

69

Glimmer said to Martha as he helped her into the rowboat. Martha winced, and her father realised she'd been hurt. 'I'm taking you right to Dr Marsh's.'

He hugged Martha, and she felt truly happy in spite of her arm and her waterlogged clothes. Her father seemed back to his old self, and she almost let out a whoop of joy. But then she noticed Mr McGill. He was green and sorrowful, like a seasick man.

'My boys,' Mr McGill moaned. 'Where have they gone?'

It took one look to know he was afraid that he and Mrs McGill had lost those they loved most in this world.

Indigo

'Don't worry,' Martha told him. 'They're the best swimmers you ever saw. They can outswim anyone.'

Charlie McGill shook his head. He didn't try to hide the fact that there were big, salty tears in his eyes.

'That's exactly what I was afraid of,' he said.

CHAPTER FOUR

Ten years earlier Charlie and Kate McGill had gone on vacation to Ocean City at just about this time of year. Though they believed they were meant to be someone's parents, they never had been and this made even the happiest times a little less happy for them. Charlie McGill always said, *What happens is what's meant to be,* and Kate McGill always nodded and said, *I suppose that's true,* but she often had a wistful look on her face, even on vacation.

The McGills went to the boardwalk and ate ice cream, and in the evenings they strolled along the beach. Their life together wasn't what they had expected, but even without a house full of children, they could still enjoy their holiday. Kate and Charlie McGill might have gone back home to Oak Grove as they did every year, back to their quiet, childless lives, if they hadn't gone walking on the beach one windy night.

They hadn't even noticed how far they'd gone until the rain began. The storm

Indigo

surprised them, and they found themselves
stranded on a stretch of sand with waves
crashing all around. There was an
abandoned fisherman's shack on the beach,
once owned by a sailor who'd drowned in a
storm such as this, and Charlie and Kate
McGill would have made a run for it and sat
out the bad weather if Charlie hadn't heard a
woman's cries.

She was out where the shore was riddled
with rocks, where the strongest currents had
been known to pull down even the most
experienced sailors. All the same, Charlie
told his wife he had no choice. He had to
help whoever was calling from beyond the
waves. He swam as hard as he could, fighting

77

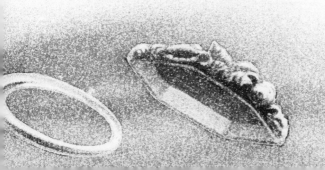

the storm and the tides, but he stopped and treaded water when he saw what had happened. A beautiful woman with long, pale hair had been gouged by the propeller of a speedboat hurrying back to the marina; whoever had captained the speedboat had been unaware of anything out in front of him other than crashing waves.

The woman's skin was iridescent, and the blood that washed into the waves and floated on the surface of the water appeared to be blue. Her strength was gone, and she was going under; she might have already given up and sunk to the depths if she hadn't had two little boys with her. Her fight to survive was strong, but she clearly couldn't

78

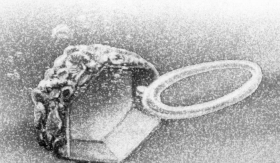

hold on much longer.

Please, she said to Charlie McGill. *Take them.* She spoke slowly, for she'd learned only bits of English from the sailor she had loved, the one who had drowned in the last storm.

Charlie McGill ferried the boys to shore, struggling against the sea, then went right back into the water to rescue their mother. By then, all he could see was the flash of a dark blue tail as she helplessly disappeared. But there, floating on a bed of seaweed, the mermaid had left something behind for her children: two beautiful rings. One was a circle of abalone shell, and one a circle of oyster shell.

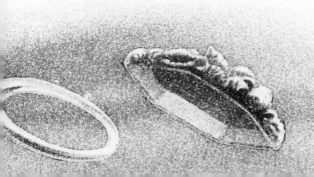

Charlie McGill took the rings and swam back to shore. On that evening, Charlie and Kate made a vow to keep the boys away from the water and to care for them all of their lives. Storms had taken both of the boys' natural parents, and the sea was always unpredictable. But try as you might to protect people from danger, you cannot keep them from their true nature.

'A mermaid's last wish is always for her children to swim free,' Charlie McGill now told Martha, 'but these boys also belong to the land.'

Hearing this story, Martha was torn. She wanted freedom and safety both for her friends. She decided that the best she could

ever hope for was that the McGill boys be granted what they longed for most of all.

By now, Trout and Eel had reached the rock wall that held back the waters. Trout had been timing himself and had found he could hold his breath underwater for more than ten minutes. This was humanly impossible, and he knew it.

'When you dream about our mother,' Eel asked, 'does she have webbing between her fingers, too?'

'She does,' Trout said.

'And between her toes?'

Trout's memory had come back in waves, helped along by the storm. The way she taught them to dive. The way she combed

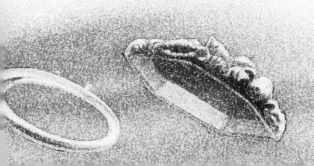

her hair with a shell. 'No toes. She had a tail, like a fish.'

Eel thought this over as they swam along. The cold water felt good on his skin. He had never had a swimming lesson in his life, and yet, like his brother, in the water he was faster and stronger than any champion. 'But we don't have tails.'

'Maybe we've lived on land too long, or maybe we're half regular old human. But we're half of whatever she was, too.'

The boys had kicked off their shoes, and the webbing between their toes gave them the streamlined glide of a porpoise. Quick as could be, they examined the stone wall that had been built to keep water out of Oak

82

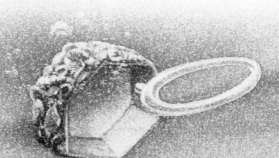

Grove and now had to be taken down to allow the floodwaters to drain. Trout knew what he had to do.

'All I need to do is pull the biggest rock out of the wall, and the rest will tumble down.'

Now that Trout understood who he really was, his green eyes were luminous. With his wet hair slicked back, he seemed more like himself. Still, he remembered that even a mermaid could have a terrible accident and drown, and he didn't want his little brother to take any chances. 'Stay here,' he told Eel. 'Don't follow me.'

Trout disappeared in the direction of the wall of stones that Charlie McGill had constructed years ago. Eel paddled around

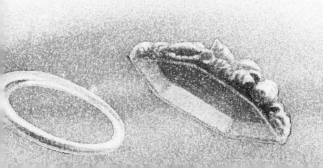

nervously. He would do anything for his brother, except this. He couldn't let Trout go on alone, so he dove underwater as well.

Eel could see surprisingly far in the muddy water. There was Trout wrestling with the largest rock in the wall. It looked as if it should have been immovable, but after a moment it creaked and tipped. Quite suddenly, it fell, dragging Trout along with it. There was a landslide of stones, and it all happened so fast, Trout hadn't time to get away.

Eel wasn't strong enough to lift the heavy stones off his brother, and yet he did. People find strength they never knew they had at certain times, and this was one of them. The

84

brothers nodded to each other, green eye to green eye. Eel used all the strength of the seas as he pulled off the stones, freeing his brother. Together, they swam to the surface, darting away from the rushing waters that could now flow out of town.

The river that Main Street had become began to drain, with wild currents and whirlpools everywhere. People on their roofs called out their approval. They cheered from whatever high ground they'd managed to find as the waters receded from basements and kitchens and roadsides alike.

One rowing boat sat bobbing in the ebbing waters like an apple in a tub. Charlie McGill stood up the moment he saw the

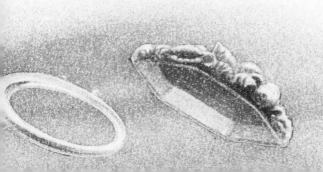

boys swimming toward him. He waved his arms and called, and if Martha and her father hadn't taken hold of his jacket, Charlie might have jumped into the water to meet Trout and Eel.

The brothers towed the rowing boat to what was not quite dry land, a muddy place they recognised as the school soccer field.

Martha jumped from the boat and hugged her friends, one after the other, with her good arm. 'You saved everyone,' she told them.

Mr Glimmer shook the boys' hands and patted their backs. But it was Charlie McGill the boys were worried about, and it was to him they turned.

Indigo

'Good work,' Charlie said.

He had never in his life been prouder than he was right now. Trout and Eel threw their muddy arms around their father.

'I thought if you got too near to water, you would swim away,' Charlie said as he held the boys close.

'We will,' Trout said.

'But then we'll swim back,' Eel added. 'We're your sons. You can never lose us.'

When the McGills got back to their muddy house, Kate McGill was waiting at the door. Kate had made a vow to take care of these boys from the day they were found in the sea, and she'd remained true to her promise. She loved them as if she were their

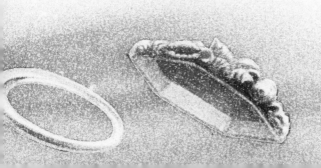

natural mother, but there was someone else who had loved them, too. For all these years Kate McGill had been waiting to give the boys a special gift, one she'd kept stored in a box fashioned out of starfish and shells that she'd bought long ago in Ocean City. She gave Eel the ring made of abalone shell, and Trout the ring made of oyster shell, and that's when they knew they were home.

CHAPTER FIVE

Dr Marsh set Martha's broken arm that evening. His office was filled with weary, damp people who had turned their ankles in the mud or sprained their backs toting buckets of water out of their basements. Dr Marsh assured Martha that she'd soon be able to throw rocks at tin cans again, but for now she had best take it easy. Afterward, Martha and her father walked home. They waved to their neighbours, who all agreed that a clear, starry night had never looked better. Even Martha admitted that Oak Grove seemed brand new, as if the floodwaters had washed everything clean.

'I thought you had it in your head to leave Oak Grove,' Mr Glimmer said.

'I might,' Martha told him. 'Some day. But not now. When I grow up. I'll travel and see all the places where my mother used to live, but today I'll go home, and wash all this mud off, and be polite to Hildy Swoon, because that's what you want me to do.'

'I don't think that will be necessary,' Mr

Indigo

Glimmer said. 'When the storm came up, Hildy hightailed it to her mother's house up on the mountain. I don't think she'll be coming back. She's happier having things her own way.'

Unless Martha was mistaken, her father looked almost as pleased as she was by this news. Martha wanted to do a little dance, but instead she only nodded.

'Sometimes people get so lonely, they don't know what to do,' Mr Glimmer said, and Martha knew exactly what he meant. When her mother was sick, Martha often went into the yard and danced under the stars until she was too dizzy to feel anything. Now, whenever she looked at the night sky, she was reminded of her mother and she felt good and lonely all mixed up together.

'Maybe we should invite Jeanette Morton over sometime,' Martha said. 'She's lonely, too.'

While Mr Glimmer thought this over, he took the yellow shawl from his pocket. 'I found this floating by. I knew you'd want it.'

Martha hugged her father and gratefully took the shawl. After they'd cleaned the water and muck out of their house, she washed the shawl and dried it carefully. For years to come she would carry it with her whenever she danced. Her feet already felt lighter.

That night she went into the yard. With the yellow shawl held high, she danced

Indigo

beneath the stars once more. She danced until she was so dizzy she could feel everything, especially the way she missed her mother.

The McGills stayed in town until the end of the school term. They didn't decide to leave because people made fun of the brothers or because they didn't fit in. Far from it. Everyone was grateful that the boys had broken through the sea wall. This summer, people would go swimming in the refilled Penman's Creek, and every time they did they would be thankful to the McGill brothers. As for Richard Grady, he soon taught himself how to swim and began to give lessons to the younger children, who gave him the nickname of Fin, a name he

95

was proud to possess in honour of the boys who'd saved him from the flood.

The reason Charlie and Kate McGill had decided to move was because they truly understood that the boys belonged as much to the water as to the land, and because it was what Trout had always wished for – to see the ocean. The McGills sold their house and the construction company and bought a place near the cove where the fisherman had lived, where they'd found the boys.

'It doesn't seem fair,' Trout said to Martha on the boys' last night in town. They were up on the garage roof, just the two of them, for Eel was home packing. They weren't bothering to throw stones

96

Indigo

anymore. 'I get my wish, and you don't.'

Some day when Trout was all grown up, and she was, too, Martha might dance for him. Her father had agreed that she could take classes in the next town, where there was a dance school. And besides, Trout was wrong about Martha not getting her wish. Hildy Swoon was gone, after all, and Oak Grove didn't look so bad any more.

The truth was, it looked like home.

'Now that you remember your mother, do you miss her more?' Martha asked.

'I missed her, anyway,' Trout said. 'Now I just know who I'm missing.'

On the day the McGills left town, Martha

97

stood on the roof of the garage so that Trout and Eel could see her waving goodbye as they drove past. Even though her best friends were leaving, Martha felt lucky. She closed her eyes and wished them a good trip. She wished them everything they wished for themselves.

The McGills drove straight through to Ocean City. Finding the way was easy, straight over the mountains to a place they'd all been before. They reached the shore by suppertime, and as she was having her dinner with her father, Martha Glimmer could have sworn she, too, could hear the sound of the tides, an echo from the farthest sea, so deep and so blue, someone who had been there would never forget.